The Big Bad Wolf a

A Fairy Tale

Connie Lamb

The White Rose UK

The Big Bad Wolf and the Syringe

A Fairy Tale

Connie Lamb

The White Rose UK

ISBN: 979-8366499255

First published in December 2022

thewhiterose.uk

For all 'Henny Pennys' and 'Ben Cocks' around the globe.

ONCE UPON A TIME ... there was a Big Bad Wolf who lived on the outskirts of Henton. He was especially renowned for going after old Granny hens and young chicks. The story of Little Red Riding Hood only made him even more unpopular.

The story of Little Red Riding Hood only made him even more unpopular.

In fact, the Henton hens avoided him wherever possible. They stayed clear of his shed where he sold pills in a shop named BBW (as in Big

Bad Wolf), and never bought any of his products.

One day, he had had enough of being the Bad Guy. Not, that he had changed... oh no. Not in the least! All that had changed was the way he wanted to lure hens into his trap. The hens didn't trust him, and that had to change. He needed a new strategy, otherwise he would never get to taste a granny or a little chick ever again.

"I want hens to *trust* me," he said.

After pondering over this, he came up with a good idea, (actually it was a *bad* idea, but he thought it rather cunning).

Firstly, he needed someone else on board. Sly Fox would be a good match, he decided. (Sly Fox was an old friend of Big Bad Wolf and true to his name, was very sly, always up to some trick or other).

"Count me in!" said Sly Fox, when he heard about the Big Bad Wolf's plan.

"Count me in!" said Sly Fox.

This was the plan: Sly Fox was to spread the word in Henton about the outbreak of a severe illness called Henflu. He was to convince the hens that if they wanted to survive, they'd have to go to the only place which offered a cure: BBW's shop!

"Needless to say, you'll get a fair share of the prey," Big Bad Wolf promised. "Just imagine how much food there'll be if every hen and cock in Henton comes round for their injection! You'll be able to choose the fattest, juiciest hens for yourself, and there will be plenty for both of us," he sneered.

SLY FOX went to the Mayor of Henton, Henna Hen, to report on the outbreak.

She was, however, sceptical. "How do I know it's true?" she clucked.

"How do I know it's true?"
Henna Hen asked.

"Just look at this," Sly Fox said. He opened his laptop, displayed a video entitled *Hens Are Dropping*

Dead In The Streets Of Chickenham!
and pressed 'play'. Henna Hen
stared at the screen: Chickenham
was only ten miles away from
Henton.

"Good grief! It's true!" she ex-
claimed, without having first
checked if the video was authentic.
(Big Bad Wolf and Sly Fox had in
fact paid a couple of actor hens to
enact the scene).

"What shall we do? I don't won't
us to catch Henflu!" she cackled.

"Well," said Sly Fox (he had
already prepared an answer): "I'm a
scientist, and I've been studying
the science, which says that staying
at home will prevent you from getting ill … in other words: If you

want Henton to stay safe, you have to stay in your pen."

"I will instantly make an announcement for all of Henton to stay indoors!"

"Way to go!" said Sly Fox, smiling and thinking of roast chicken.

A FRAID OF CATCHING HENFLU, the hens of Henton stayed obediently at home. However, after six days, they got terribly bored from being locked up in their pens all day long. "We need to get out and about, and live our lives..." they complained to the Mayor of

Henton. "This lockdown is going on for ever!"

Mayor Henna Hen rang up Sly Fox—she felt she could trust him now. "Listen, Sly Fox," she said. "Thank you so much for caring for us all. I truly appreciate it! But the hens are going mad in their pens. They need to get out. They're getting angry at me for keeping them inside. And to be honest, between you and me, I haven't seen any hens dying of Henflu yet."

"Alright," said Sly Fox. Again, he was prepared for this. "Your hens can leave their pens. But don't think Henflu is over. It's as life-threatening as ever! Whoever leaves home, must cover their beak and nose to stay safe. That will prevent everyone from infecting each other."

"Thank you! Thank you, Sly Fox. That sounds very sensible. I'm so glad we can all go out now," replied Henna Hen.

"No big deal. And remember: BEAK, NOSE, MASK!" Sly Fox added before hanging up.

"How caring and thoughtful he is," Henna Hen reflected on her phone call. "I will tell everyone to mask up now, and anyone who doesn't, will be punished!"

So every (well, *almost* every) hen and cock of Henton masked up. They were really happy to be allowed out of their pens. They didn't mind the mask-wearing if this meant freedom. However, after some time, the masks became more and more of a nuisance. For some, it kept slipping off; others were getting aggressive because they couldn't breathe well. Behind the mask, clucking sounded awful and it was difficult to understand one another.

Then disaster struck. Hen Sally Monella was overweight and suffered from a heart failure, which made her puff and pant, even without a mask. But wearing a mask was just about the last straw. One day she collapsed and was found dead. Nothing could be done to revive her.

The incident was all over the Henton News Show. But what they said in the report was simply not true...

After talking about the mysterious disappearance of freezers in Henton (which caused the Lack of Freezers Crisis, aka LFC) reporter Cock Crow said in a very serious voice: "Hen Sally Monella has died of ... *Henflu!*"

All the hens were aflutter.

"Hen Sally Monella has died of ... Henflu!"

MAYOR HENNA HEN rang up Sly Fox once more. "These masks aren't working!" she complained. "My people are dropping dead of Hen-flu."

"Wearing a mask is now more

important than ever!" Sly Fox countered. "You all have to wear it to prevent more hens from dropping dead! As a scientist, I recommend wearing *two* masks..."

Henna Hen hung up the telephone angrier than before. But she wasn't angry at Sly Fox. Oh, no. He was such a sensible, clever scientist. She was angry at all those who weren't wearing a mask. It was time for a clear-up.

"Anyone caught without a mask has to pay a fine of £600!" she threatened on the evening Henton News Show. "No mask, no entry. Do you hear? Stop putting your Granny's life at risk!"

Meanwhile, more and more hens

suffered under their mask (or masks, if they wore two) because they had *too little air to breathe*, and more were suddenly collapsing.

Whenever a hen or cock appeared without a mask, which was rare, panic broke out. The unmasked got pointed at, screamed at and chased out of shops, buses, libraries or wherever they happened to be. A hen without mask was like a ticking, walking bomb.

You see, hens could get quite nasty when challenged.

AND IT GOT EVEN WORSE...

Mayor Henna Hen was completely convinced that Sly Fox was a good guy who only wanted the best for her and the rest of Henton. Because now he even offered a considerable amount of money, if she would just comply and recite a script on the Henton News Show (the script was actually written by Big Bad Wolf, but never mind).

"Dear inhabitants of Henton," Mayor Henna Hen began, while gleefully imagining her bank account overflowing with funds. "I would like to thank all those who have done the Right Thing and stayed in their pens when told, and worn a mask to stop infection..." She quickly slipped on a mask to ensure that she looked compliant and carried on dutifully: "Now our Manufacture of Medicine, BBW [she didn't mention Big Bad Wolf's full name because that might induce wrong ideas] has invented a cure! Soon we won't need to be locked down, or wear a mask anymore because the new cure will save us all from Henflu and lead to freedom. This cure—it's an injection—is a miracle cure! Line up today to get your injection!"

All the hens and cocks, except for the unmasked bullied ones, cheered.

"What brilliant news! Freedom at

last!" they shouted in front of their TVs and radios.

The hens and cocks of Henton queued at the BBW shed.

Soon the hens and cocks of Henton queued at the BBW shed where they were kindly met by Big Bad Wolf holding a *big* syringe. One after the other they got their shot. All on the same day.

But strangely, after being injected, they didn't seem to come out of the shed again.

HENNY PENNY was one of the unmasked and bullied hens. She watched with horror as her friends, neighbours and relatives left to queue in front of BBW.

"Don't take the shot—it's not necessary and it might be toxic," she told people. But no-one listened.

Then she noticed something strange. "Nobody's coming back," she told her best friend, Ben Cock.

"People are simply disappearing after the shot!"

"This needs investigating," Ben Cock said, and together they went to BBW. The queue was still very long.

They sneaked to the back of the shed. There was a fenced area behind the shed, and between the laths this is what they saw: A pile of dead hens on the gras! Every few minutes another dead hen was flung to the back and landed on the pile of lifeless poultry. It was the worst scene Henny Penny and Ben Cock had ever caught sight of in their whole life.

They ran back to the queue and warned people of what they had seen with their own eyes. But most hens just looked away. Henny Penny and Ben Cock ran to the town centre of Henton, and grabbed a megaphone.

"Don't go to BBW! You'll get killed!" they shouted to the hens and cocks that were getting on buses and into cars to drive there.

"Put a mask on, you granny-killers!" came an angry muffled response from a masked driver. Most hens just ignored them.

It was devastating!

Meanwhile the death pile behind the BBW shed grew, and only Henny Penny, Ben Cock and a few others knew about this.

THE GOOD NEWS is, a few thens *did* listen to Henny Penny and Ben Cock. They turned away from the queue or didn't go there in the first place.

Henny Penny, Ben Cock and their unmasked, bullied allies also survived that dark day. And believe me, they never *ever* trusted a Big Bad Wolf with a syringe!

They never trusted a Big Bad Wolf with a syringe.

Aftermath

MAYOR HENNA HEN survived too. Not because she was clever enough to see through the deceit, no, it was because she missed her BBW appointment through being distracted with counting her extra money.

After the whole thing blew up, Henna Hen felt foolish for believing Sly Fox. Despite showing remorse, she was convicted of High Treason and Henslaughter and was locked up for life in Hen Prison.

Henna Hen in Hen Prison.

Big Bad Wolf and Sly Fox fled the area when their fraud became obvious. They had gathered enough food for the coming years. Now you may understand why all freezers had disappeared in Henton. It's because they had planned to use them for storing chicken!

After aftermath

Big Bad Wolf and Sly Fox then retreated to luxury estates in South America. The two baddies fell out with each and became enemies. Sly Fox accused Big Bad Wolf of taking the greater share of poultry, even though he (Sly Fox) had done more work. Big Bad Wolf said that it was a fair share because, after all, everything was thanks to *his* plan.

They both became overweight and unhealthy from scoffing too much greasy roast chicken.

They scoffed too much greasy roast chicken.

And believe it or not, during one of their fights, they both dropped off the edge of a deep ravine, never to be seen again!

As for brave Henny Penny and Ben Cock - well, they moved to the beautiful countryside and watched the sunrise and sunset each day.

They looked after their chicks, pecked their grain, drank clean spring water, and lived happily ever after.

The End.

Henny Penny and Ben Cock watching the sunrise.

Other Books

Hope Amidst a Tsunami of Evil—Exposing the Great Lies. Veronica Finch, September 2022, 250 pages.

Evidence, facts, essays, testimonies, letters and reflections.

The White Rose—Defending Freedom. Veronica Finch, November 2021, 102 pages.

All about the White Rose UK, including English translations of flyers from the German underground resistance.

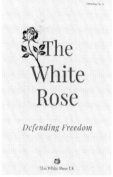

Freedom!—An Anthology of Poems, Short Stories and Essays. Various authors, March 2021, 147 pages.

Composed by 36 authors questioning Covid restrictions and lockdowns.

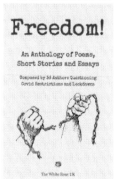

➢ Order more books online: thewhiterose.uk/white-rose-products
➢ Visit thewhiterose.uk to view over 1,700 articles for free.
➢ Sign up to our free weekly newsletter: thewhiterose.uk/newsletter

Printed in Great Britain
by Amazon

13375148R00021